This book belongs to

....

This is a story about Snow White,

You can read it by day or read it at night!

There's something else. Can you guess what?

Throughout this book there's a robin to spot.

This edition first published in 2010 by Castle Street Press
an imprint of make believe ideas ltd.

Text copyright © 2006 Nick and Claire Page
Copyright © 2006 make believe ideas ltd
27 Castle Street, Berkhamsted, Hertfordshire, HP4 2DW, UK.
565, Royal Parkway, Nashville, TN 37214, USA.

Snow White

Nick and Claire Page

Illustrations by Bee Willey

Once there was a young princess,
with skin as white as snow,
lips as red as blood, and
hair as black as ebony.
She was called Snow White.

Her mother was dead and her
father had married again.
The new queen was beautiful
but vain. Every day she asked:
"Mirror, mirror on the wall,
who is the fairest of them all?"
And the mirror replied:
"You, O Queen, are the fairest,
it's true. No one else looks as
good as you."

Each year, Snow White grew
more beautiful. One day, the
queen said to her mirror:
"Mirror, mirror on the wall,
who is the fairest of them all?"

The mirror answered:
"You, O Queen, are a lovely sight,
but if you force me to choose,
I'll go for Snow White."
The queen turned yellow with
shock, then green with envy.

She ordered a huntsman to take Snow White into the forest and kill her. But the huntsman felt sorry for Snow White and let her go. She ran through the forest, until she came to a tiny house.

Inside, there was a table with seven places and seven little beds. Snow White lay on the beds and fell asleep.

Later, seven dwarfs came home from digging in the mines. They were surprised to find Snow White in their home!

"Who are you?" she asked.
"We are Monday, Tuesday,
Wednesday, Thursday, Friday,
Saturday, and Fred," they said.

The dwarfs agreed to let Snow
White stay to look after the
house and cook their meals.

Back at the palace, the
queen asked again:
"Mirror, mirror on the wall,
who is the fairest of them all?"

And the mirror replied:
"You, O Queen, have the beauty
of night. But you still come
second to Princess Snow White.
She's still alive and still
good-looking. She lives with the
dwarfs and does their cooking."

The Queen turned purple with passion and red with rage.

The queen used her magic.
She disguised herself as an old
woman and went to the cottage:
"Try my apples. Take a bite!
They are just the thing for skin
so white!"

Snow White didn't know it was
the queen, so she bought a juicy
red apple. But the apple was
poisoned. When Snow White took
a bite, she fell down, as if dead.

The dwarfs found Snow
White lying on the ground.
"She's dead!" cried Monday,
Tuesday, Wednesday, Thursday,
Friday, Saturday, and Fred.

They put her in a glass coffin
and took turns to guard it.

Have you
seen this Woman?

Guard Duty
Monday ..... Wednesday
Tuesday ..... Friday
Wednesday .... Saturday
Thursday ..... Monday
Friday ..... Tuesday
Saturday ..... Fred
Sunday ....

The queen ran back to
the palace.
"Mirror, mirror on the wall,
who is the fairest of them all?"

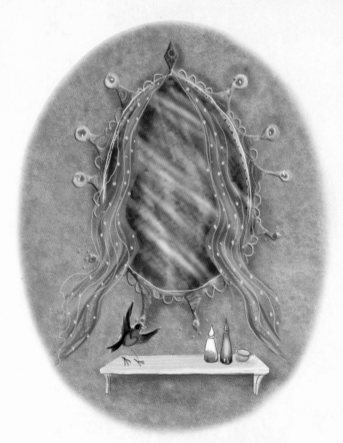

And the mirror replied, sadly:
"You, O Queen, are the fairest
of fair. Snow White's dead, so
what do I care?"

One day, a prince came riding through the forest. He saw Snow White and fell in love at once. "Let me take her to my castle," he said. "I cannot live without her."

As his servants lifted the coffin, the piece of poisoned apple fell out of Snow White's mouth.

At once Snow White woke up!
"She's not dead!" cried Monday,
Tuesday, Wednesday, Thursday,
Friday, Saturday, and Fred.

Back at the castle, the queen
asked her mirror:
"Mirror, mirror, on the wall,
who is the fairest of them all?"
And the mirror answered:
"You, O Queen, are far from
plain. But Snow White is
alive again!"

The queen turned every color under the sun, all at once, and shattered into a thousand pieces.

So Snow White married the prince. And the seven dwarfs came and saw them every day: Monday, Tuesday, Wednesday, Thursday, Friday, Saturday, and Fred.

Ready to tell

Oh no! Some of the pictures from this story have been mixed up! Can you retell the story and point to each picture in the correct order?

Picture dictionary

Encourage your child to read these harder words from the story and gradually develop their basic vocabulary.

beautiful

disguised

dwarf

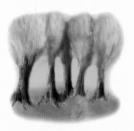
forest

mirror

palace

prince

princess

shattered

Key words

Here are some key words used in context.
Help your child to use other words from
the border in simple sentences.

Snow White **was** beautiful.

The queen did not **like** her.

The mirror **said**...

The prince saw Snow White.

They were happy.

Make a magic mirror

You may not be able to make a truly magic mirror,
but it's easy to make a mirror that's fit for a princess.

You will need

a mirror tile • sticky tape • a large sheet of cardboard
• a pencil • a ruler • paint or crayons • glue
• beads, feathers, toy jewels and pieces of tissue paper

What to do

1 Take care! Some tiles have sharp edges. Ask a grown-up
to put tape around the edges to make them safe.
2 Carefully lay the tile on the middle
of the cardboard and draw round it.
3 Ask a grown-up to draw one line about
1 in (2.5 cm) outside the square you have
drawn, and another 1/2 in (1.5 cm) inside.
4 Cut along the two new lines to
make a simple frame. (You may
need a grown-up to help.)
5 Color the cardboard, using crayons or paint (let it dry)
Stick beads, jewels, feathers, or bits of tissue paper on one
side of the frame. Make it look really special.
6 When the glue has dried, carefully stick the tile to the
back using strong tape.
Turn it over and you have a "magic" mirror of your own!

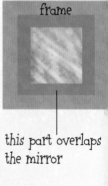

frame

this part overlaps
the mirror